# Lottie Perkins

For brilliant boys and girls everywhere.
Yes, that's you! – KN

To dearest Ari, for supporting even my
silliest of ideas – MK

 The ABC 'Wave' device is a trademark of the
Australian Broadcasting Corporation and is used
under licence by HarperCollins*Publishers* Australia.

First published in Australia in 2018
by HarperCollins*Children's Books*
a division of HarperCollins*Publishers* Australia Pty Limited
ABN 36 009 913 517
harpercollins.com.au

Text copyright © Katrina Nannestad 2018
Illustrations copyright © Makoto Koji 2018

The rights of Katrina Nannestad and Makoto Koji to be identified
as the author and illustrator of this work have been asserted by them
in accordance with the *Copyright Amendment (Moral Rights) Act 2000*.

This work is copyright. Apart from any use as permitted under the
*Copyright Act 1968*, no part may be reproduced, copied, scanned, stored
in a retrieval system, recorded, or transmitted, in any form or by any
means, without the prior written permission of the publisher.

**HarperCollins***Publishers*
Level 13, 201 Elizabeth Street, Sydney NSW 2000, Australia
Unit D1, 63 Apollo Drive, Rosedale, Auckland 0632, New Zealand
A 53, Sector 57, Noida, UP, India
1 London Bridge Street, London SE1 9GF, United Kingdom
2 Bloor Street East, 20th floor, Toronto, Ontario M4W 1A8, Canada
195 Broadway, New York NY 10007, USA

A catalogue record for this book is available
from the National Library of Australia

ISBN 978 0 7333 3906 6 (paperback)
ISBN 978 0 7333 3910 3 (library edition)

Cover and internal design by Hazel Lam, HarperCollins Design Studio
Typeset in Bembo Infant by Kirby Jones
Sticker insert printed in China by RR Donnelley
Printed and bound in Australia by McPherson's Printing Group
The papers used by HarperCollins in the manufacture of this book are
a natural, recyclable product made from wood grown in sustainable
plantation forests. The fibre source and manufacturing processes meet
recognised international environmental standards, and carry certification.

# Lottie Perkins

## BALLERINA

### BY KATRINA NANNESTAD
### ILLUSTRATED BY MAKOTO KOJI

ABC Books

# CHAPTER 1

My name is Charlotte Perkins.
My friends call me LOTTIE.

I'm an exceptional child.

I'm good at tying ribbons into bows.

I'm good at making my shoes squeak on shiny floors.

I'm good at balancing on garden walls.

I'm good at handling snails.

'You are an exceptional child, Lottie Perkins,' I say to myself. 'And don't let anyone tell you otherwise.'

'Charlotte Perkins, you are a MENACE,' says Mr O'Hara.

Mr O'Hara is our next-door

neighbour. He invites my mother

to come in for a chat.

A serious chat.

About all the flowers I've picked

from his garden.

I'm good at sneaking away from spots of bother. I creep along Mr O'Hara's hallway, out the front door, past his sleeping dog Brutus and through the gate.

Mum doesn't even hear me go. Nor does Brutus.

Which proves that I'm also good at walking on my tippy-toes.

'You are exceptionally light on your toes, Lottie Perkins,' I say to myself. 'You should be a BALLERINA!'

# CHAPTER 2

'I'm going to be a ballerina!' I tell Mr O'Hara.

'Get down off my garden wall!' he snaps.

I tippy-toe along the wall until I fall.

I fall down into the flowerbed.

Right on top of Mr O'Hara's tulips.

'GRRR!' says Brutus. That's dog talk for, 'Good try, Lottie. Practice makes perfect.'

'I'm going to be a ballerina!' I tell my class.

'Don't be a PEANUT BRAIN,' says Harper Dark. 'You look like a mud wrestler, not a ballerina.'

Harper Dark is a bully and a kill-joy.

I want to show her she's wrong.

I stand up on my tippy-toes and pirouette like a real ballerina. I spin around and around. Until I get dizzy and crash into Mrs Dawson's desk.

🎀 🎀 🎀

'I'm going to be a ballerina!' I tell my best friend, Sam Bell.

'Supersonic sausage dogs!' shouts Sam. 'Great timing!'

Sam drags me across the street

and points to a poster outside the town hall.

> # BELLA BALLET COMPANY
> performs *Swan Lake*.
> **ONE NIGHT ONLY.**
> Local children welcome to audition.

'You should try out, Lottie!' Sam smiles. 'You'll get in for sure.'

And *that's* why Sam is my best friend. He's kind and funny and helpful and says crazy things like, 'Supersonic sausage dogs!'

And he BELIEVES in me.

# CHAPTER 3

I'm wearing a yellow tutu and a sparkly tiara. They are from my dress-up box.

I pirouette for my pet goat, Feta. Three times. And I don't even trip.

'How do I look?' I ask.

'BAA!' says Feta. That's goat

talk for, 'Perfect! Except for the sneakers.'

I flit on tippy-toes all the way to my bedroom.

I stand before the mirror and hum the tune from *Swan Lake*.

I cup my hands in front of my tummy. I point my knees and toes outwards and bob slowly up and down.

I lift my hands and leap about the room like a gazelle.

I tuck my hands behind my back and balance on one foot. I hold the pose and smile at my imaginary audience. Even though I can feel something tugging at my tutu.

Because a true ballerina needs to focus on her art.

'Well done, Lottie Perkins,' I say to myself. 'You are an exceptional ballerina.'

'BAA!' says Feta. That's goat talk for, 'Delicious! Light and fluffy, like a meringue!'

Feta has just eaten the skirt off the back of my tutu!

# CHAPTER 4

The town hall is BUZZING. Everyone wants to audition for the ballet.

Except for Sam. He wants to work backstage.

Harper Dark is here, wearing a pink tutu and proper ballet shoes.

Pretty pink ribbons crisscross up to her knees. Her hair is pulled back into a perfect bun.

Harper stares at my scruffy tutu and sneakers. She rolls her eyes and nudges Eve Roberts in the side. Eve giggles.

My cheeks burn and my legs feel wobbly. Ballerinas need strong legs.

'Don't worry, Lottie,' whispers Sam. 'It's all about TALENT, not tutus.'

He's right!

I flash him a brave smile
and remind myself that I am an
exceptional child.

Madame Mimi claps her hands.
The piano begins to play.

Girls and boys tippy-toe across the stage, as light as butterflies. Everyone stops and stares. My sneakers are squeaking!

The music changes. Children leap and fly and sashay across the stage. I leap too far and crash into Raj Singh. His nose bleeds. His big sister yells at me.

'PIROUETTE!' cries Madame Mimi.

I close my eyes and spin. Faster and faster.

Until I get tangled in the curtains at the edge of the stage.

Madame Mimi mops her brow.

'I think I've seen enough,' she says.

# CHAPTER 5

My legs jitter. My toes twitch.

Madame Mimi is reading out the list. The list of children who will perform in *Swan Lake*.

'First Little Swan – HARPER DARK!'

Harper Dark squeals and fans her face. She runs up onto the stage. She bows and blows kisses to everyone. First Little Swan is the BEST role of all.

Soon, Harper is joined by nine other children, all Little Swans.

My heart sinks. My shoulders slump.

I've missed out.

I trudge across the hall.

I'm almost out the door when Sam grabs me by the hand.

'Wait, Lottie!' shouts Sam. 'YOU GOT IN!'

🎀 🎀 🎀

I, Lottie Perkins, have been given the role of First Tree. I don't know whether to be happy or horrified.

'First Tree?' I gasp.

'*Only* tree,' says Sam. 'But there's

a proper costume and you still get to be onstage.'

Sam's right. I make a choice, there and then.

I stand up tall and smile.

'I'm going to be the best dancing tree ever!' I cry.

# CHAPTER 6

Trees don't dance. They don't even MOVE.

I stand onstage, stuck inside a giant wooden tree. Only my face can be seen through a hole in the trunk.

Harper Dark dances past, gloating.

'You must be *so* embarrassed,' she says.

Harper is wearing the most beautiful costume I have ever seen. It's a white tutu with a skirt made entirely of feathers. Big, fluffy

white feathers. On her head is a tiara made of pearls. Her ballet shoes are white with silver ribbons.

SILVER ribbons!

I watch ten Little Swans flit and leap and pirouette across the stage.

I could have danced like that.

I just needed a little more practice.

It's break time. I'm freed from the tree.

I stretch my arms and legs.

I look around to make sure no-one is watching, then I dance. I flit and leap and pirouette, as though I am First Little Swan in *Swan Lake*.

'You are a HOPELESS ballerina!' snaps Harper Dark.

Harper has been spying on me from behind the curtains! Three Little Swans peep out beside her.

They are all giggling.

At me.

'You should stick to being a tree,' says Harper. 'A big, stupid, ugly TREE.'

# CHAPTER 7

'I'm going to be the most beautiful and talented tree ever,' I say.

'Good for you, Lottie!' cries Sam. 'I'll help in any way I can.'

'Thank you,' I say. 'I need some snails.'

I hand him an empty jam jar.

I creep around Mr O'Hara's garden, picking flowers. Lots and lots of flowers.

As I go, I hum the music from *Swan Lake*. I imagine I am First Little Swan. I sashay across the daffodils. I leap over the tulips. I pirouette through the violets.

'GRRR!' says Brutus, baring his fangs. That's dog talk for,

'You're a wonderful ballerina, Lottie Perkins.'

'I know,' I say. 'But for now, I am a tree and I just have to make the best of things.'

I bath Feta and blow-dry her hair.

Feta hates baths. I feed her a cake of soap and she forgives me. She'd like to eat the rubber duck, but I keep it for myself.

# CHAPTER 8

Sam, Feta and I arrive at the town hall early. We tie bunches of flowers all over the tree. Sam climbs a ladder and sits the rubber duck in the highest branch. I tie Feta to the trunk and plop live snails on the leaves.

We stand back and admire our work.

'PICKLE MY PANTS!' cries Sam. 'You'll be the best tree ever, Lottie.'

While we wait for the others to arrive, Sam plays the piano. It's just 'Chopsticks', but I don't mind. A good ballerina can dance to any tune.

I dance the part of First Little Swan. I tippy-toe and flit.

I sashay and leap. I pirouette like a spinning top.

'What a goose!' shouts Harper Dark.

Sam stops playing.

I stop spinning.

All ten Little Swans are standing in front of the stage, smirking at me.

My cheeks burn. My eyes sting.

Harper stomps up the stairs.

'This is how *you* dance, POTTIE LERKINS,' she says.

Harper plods and limps across the stage.

She spins and wobbles, her arms and legs thrashing all over the place.

She goes cross-eyed and lets her tongue hang out to one side.

She grunts and heaves and leaps.

She slips on a runaway snail and tumbles off the stage.

CRACK!

Harper has broken her leg.

# CHAPTER 9

'Tragedy!' cries Madame Mimi.

'We must cancel the ballet.'

'What if we find a NEW First Little Swan?' asks Sam.

Madame Mimi ponders the idea.

'It would need to be someone who knows all of the steps,' she says.

'Someone who has practised day and night.'

Madame Mimi scratches her head.

Feta eats a snail.

Three Little Swans weep.

'Butter my boots!' shouts Sam. 'I know JUST the person!'

# CHAPTER 10

I stand in the wings, butterflies in my tummy, joy in my heart.

I'm wearing a white tutu with a skirt made entirely of feathers. Big, fluffy white feathers. On my head is a tiara made of pearls.

My ballet shoes are white with silver ribbons. I have tied them in perfect bows beneath my knees.

I look across at the tree. It no longer looks beautiful. The flowers are wilting. Feta has eaten the rubber duck. And the face that stares from the hole in the trunk is UGLY with rage.

Harper Dark is First Tree.

The orchestra begins to play.

Sam opens the red velvet curtains.

The spotlight beams.

This is it! Bella Ballet Company presents *Swan Lake*.

I flit across the stage on my tippy-toes. Nine Little Swans follow. Our feathers flutter as we glide around the silver lake. Swan Lake.

The audience sighs in delight.

I pirouette to the front of the stage and wave my hand.

I am First Little Swan.

I am the HAPPIEST ballerina in the world.

THE END

Look like a BALLERINA.
Choose at least four of these
things to wear or hold:

- a pink leotard
- pink ballet slippers
- pink tights
- pink leg warmers
- a bag of pink marshmallows (ballet dancing uses a lot of energy)
- a giant pink tote bag
- a white tutu with a skirt made of feathers
- white ballet shoes with silver ribbons
- a pearl tiara
- a bun (in your hair, not your lunchbox)

# COLLECT THEM ALL!